Frog Went A-Traveling

A RUSSIAN FOLKTALE

retold by Amanda StJohn • illustrated by David Wenzel

The Child's World

Distributed by The Child's World®
1980 Lookout Drive • Mankato, MN 56003-1705
800-599-READ • www.childsworld.com

Acknowledgments
The Child's World®: Mary Berendes, Publishing Director
The Design Lab: Kathleen Petelinsek, Design
Red Line Editorial: Editorial direction

Library of Congress Cataloging-in-Publication Data
StJohn, Amanda, 1982–
   Frog went a-traveling : a Russian folktale / by Amanda StJohn ;
illustrated by David Wenzel.
        p. cm.
   Summary: In Siberia, Fedya the frog convinces a flock of Squawk ducks
to give her a ride when they fly south, but her determination to let people
know the flight was her idea nearly costs Fedya her life. Includes notes
about folk tales and about Russia.
   ISBN 978-1-60973-136-6 (library reinforced : alk. paper)
   [1. Folklore—Russia.] I. Wenzel, David, 1950– ill. II. Title.
   PZ8.1.S8577Frr 2012
   398.20947'045–dc23   2011010890

Printed in the United States of America in Mankato, Minnesota.
July 2011
PA02086

ome, listen. I have a tale from the beautiful Siberian swamps and marshes of Russia. Frogs and ducks meet one another in such wetlands, as they do in this very story.

There once was a clever Siberian wood frog named Fedja. Russians say it like this: *FED-ya*. Fedja invented a new way for frogs to travel. But she wanted the whole world to know that the idea was hers alone. That pride nearly cost the frog her life. . . .

Have you ever wished that you could fly? Fedja was a frog who wished to travel far, far from home—all by herself. But Fedja knew it was dangerous to hop away from her marsh because she might be gobbled up.

So Fedja went to a quiet place to dream up a better way to travel. "I know!" she said. "If frogs could fly, we could travel more safely than on land."

Fedja's brother chuckled at her. "*Kva-kva-kva.* Frogs can't fly!"

Fedja pretended not to hear her brother. She simply turned her back to him and began her work. First, Fedja made a pair of flashy wings out of leaves and sticks.

She leaped into the air and glided in dazzling spirals. "Look at me!" Fedja croaked.

"Uf!" She crashed into a tree, and her brother chuckled.

Next, Fedja built a slingshot out of a forked tree branch and some reeds. Fedja leaned back into the reeds. She was sure she could sling herself all the way to China. Fedja stretched the sling back as far as it would go.

"Hey! Watch this!" she croaked and lifted her feet.

"Uf." Instead of slinging her to China, the reeds broke. Fedja splashed into the marsh. She could hear her brother laughing nearby. Her heart felt as heavy as mud.

Just then, a flock of thirsty squawk
ducks landed in the marsh—*psshhh!*

Underwater, Fedja watched the ducks
and listened very closely.

"Whew! It's getting cold out!" said
one duck.

"We'd better fly south quickly,"
said another.

"Did you say *fly?*" Fedja appeared atop a lily pad. She bowed before the ducks. "I'm Fedja, the flying frog," she announced. "I want to come with you to the south."

Wot-wot-wot, laughed the ducks. "Frogs can't fly!"

"Allow me to come up with a plan, will you?" Fedja pleaded.

When the ducks promised to wait, Fedja slipped beneath the lily pad and made her greatest plan yet.

"Brrr! Time to go," said a duck. "It's getting colder."

"Wait!" Fedja appeared with something hidden behind her back. "Ta-da!" She revealed an ordinary stick.

"We will have to work together," said Fedja. "But two of you ducks can hold on to this stick with your bills. I will hold on to the middle with my mouth, and you can carry me."

The Squawk ducks made a private huddle. The idea sounded fun, but they knew that the frog was heavy. Two ducks would grow tired after carrying her for a short time.

"Our flock is large," said a colorful duck. "What if we take turns holding the stick?"

"Then, no one would get tired," said another.

"*Da.* Yes, we will take you south to China," said the colorful duck.

When everyone was ready, two ducks held on to the stick with their bills. Fedja wrapped her mouth around the stick, and everyone took off.

"Mmm! Mmmm!" Fedja was quite scared at first. Her tummy fluttered as the ducks carried her higher and higher. Still, she did not let go of the stick with her mouth.

"I've never seen such a brave frog!" said an old duck.

"How remarkable!" said a mama duck.

Fedja really wanted to say thank you. She liked the compliment and was proud of herself for figuring out how to fly. But, not wanting to fall, Fedja remained silent.

Fedja took in the amazing view below her dangling feet. From the sky, Russia looked very large, and also very small. Fedja saw mountains, long ribbons of water, and trees as green as frogs. She saw small villages, where goats trotted along dirt roads and people looked up at the ducks.

Hello, can you see me? Fedja didn't dare say this aloud, but she thought it. Then, Fedja became worried and upset. *What if the people think that the ducks were the ones who figured out how to carry me? I must do something about this!*

The ducks came to rest along the banks of a river. While they ate their fill of water plants, Fedja went to a quiet place to think.

Soon the ducks were ready to fly away. Fedja stopped them and said, "I felt a little queasy the last time we flew. If I get sick, I'll let go of the stick and fall. Could you fly lower to the ground?"

"Sure, sure," they said, and everyone took off.

The ducks flew very low over the land, and Fedja eagerly awaited the attention of the villagers. Finally, a little girl looked up and pointed at the flock. "Look, Mama."

All the villagers came running after the ducks to see the flying frog. "Those ducks are carrying a frog!" they cheered. "Isn't that clever?"

Fedja became enraged. *No, no,* she thought. *It wasn't their idea. It was my idea!*

"Look at those witty squawk ducks," a father said to his child.

Fedja could take it no longer. She forgot about holding on to the stick and opened her mouth. "I am Fedja, the flying frog. This was all my idea!"

"Oh, noooooo!" Fedja tumbled from the sky. The ducks swooped to catch her, but she fell too quickly.

"Uf." Fedja landed in a muddy pond with a splash. She was as red as a beet with embarrassment. "How could I have forgotten that I would fall if I spoke?"

Fedja never got to see China. And because her new home was just a tiny pond, large flocks of ducks did not stop for food. Once in a while, children from town came to visit her, but Fedja pursed her lips shut. She said nothing about her wonderful travels as the flying frog because she didn't want to people to know how it ended.

FOLKTALES

Frog *Went A-Traveling* is an example of a Russian folktale. In Russian, the word for folktale is *skazka*, which means, "that which is told." In essence, it is a story people tell to others.

When one story is told many times by lots of different people in a community, it becomes common knowledge—or something that nearly everyone knows by heart. Eventually, someone will want to write the story down—that way, it will never be forgotten. Even if people move to a new state or country, they can learn about the stories of their homeland.

Siberia is a place in eastern Russia that is so large, it takes up more than half of the country. Siberia is a gorgeous wilderness with mountains, forests, rivers, marshes, and swamps. Still, most Russians don't live in Siberia. The weather is usually either frightfully cold or terribly wet. It can be difficult to travel and to grow food in Siberia.

But some animals thrive in Siberia's extreme conditions, including Siberian wood frogs such as Fedja. Squawk ducks, also known as Baikal teals, also make Siberia their habitat. Both of these frogs and ducks are also found in countries south of Russia, such as Mongolia and China.

ABOUT THE ILLUSTRATOR

David Thorn Wenzel has illustrated many children's books, and each one has given him an opportunity to explore another time or place. David is best recognized for his illustrated graphic novel of J.R.R. Tolkien's, *The Hobbit*, and for his rendition of the holiday classic *Rudolph The Red Nosed Reindeer*. David was honored to continue Maurice Sendak's, "Little Bear" series in over twelve books. The artist resides on a hill overlooking a beautiful farm valley in Connecticut. His wife Janice is an artist and a teacher, and both of David's sons—as well as his brother—are artists, too!